Text © Margaret Carter
Illustrations © Richard Fowler
First published 1993 by
Campbell Books
12 Half Moon Court · London EC1A 7HE

Printed in Hong Kong

ISBN 1 85292 156 0

Winter's Coming

Margaret Carter
Richard Fowler

CAMPBELL BOOKS

– the children played very happily in the forest –

Winter's coming.

In the middle of the great forest called Ashridge there once lived a family of bears. There was a father, a mother, two boys – Tim and George – and the baby, who was called Daisy.

During summer the children played very happily in the forest but when the leaves on the trees turned from green to red and yellow, they knew winter was coming.

'We must get ready for the cold weather,' Mother Bear would say.

Then she would make the children try on their wellies to see that they didn't let in water, and she would try on their woolly hats to see if they still fitted.

Mostly they didn't, of course, and very funny they looked too!

'Oh dear!' Mother Bear would say.

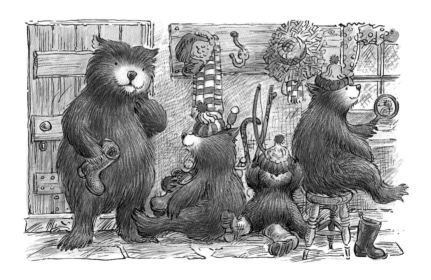

But what the children liked best of all
was helping father to collect wood for
the winter fires.

Every day they would ask 'Shall we get
the wood today, father?' And every day
he would reply 'Soon, children, soon!'

And then one morning, after breakfast, he
put down his newspaper, looked out of the
window and said 'I think we'll see how much
wood there is left in the shed.'

'Hooray!' cried both boys together.

Now the shed was very dark inside and a bit scary. At first they couldn't see anything and then they heard a very faint noise . . . *'rustle, rustle'* it went.

'Help!' said George. 'Goodness!' said Tim and in case it was something quite dreadful they both got behind father.

Two bright eyes were shining through the darkness. Slowly a face grew round the eyes. It was a dormouse!

'Why Dormouse,' said George, 'whatever are you doing here?' 'I'm making my winter nest,' yawned Dormouse. 'Soon I shall curl myself into a ball, chin on tummy, very warm and cosy and there I'll sleep until the daffodils are blooming.'

And with a last yawn he scampered off.

Father had been looking at the logs left from last year. 'We'll need a lot more than these' he said. 'Get the sledge out, boys.'

'And here's your picnic' called mother.

They ate every scrap and shared the last crumbs with the birds.

As Daisy couldn't walk very fast, they gave her a ride on the sledge and very soon they came to a great beech tree that had fallen in the storms. 'Just right for us,' said father and while he chopped at the branches the boys piled the logs on the sledge. Daisy sat and watched them.

For some time they all worked very hard and soon the sledge was almost full.

At last father stopped, mopping his brow. 'Let's have our picnic' he said.

The food was delicious: hot soup, buns and sausages, apples and honey cakes. They ate every scrap and shared the last crumbs with the birds.

Then suddenly 'Ooo!' cried Daisy.

She was rubbing her head and pointing
to an acorn in the grass.

'It must have fallen from the tree,'
said Tim. 'But oh Daisy it can't have
hurt you at all – it's very small.'

'Back to work, boys,' said father, but
George stayed behind, looking up at the
tree. A pair of bright eyes was looking
down at him. 'You threw that nut, Squirrel,' he
whispered. 'But I won't tell!' And he was smiling
as he ran to join the others.

Naughty George.

George was getting very tired of helping his father and brother to collect wood for their winter fires.

'Isn't it time to go home yet?' he asked, rather sadly.

'Nearly,' said Father Bear. 'I just want to finish chopping this last branch.'

'If you'd help a bit more,' grumbled Tim, 'we could get home sooner.'

But George didn't answer. He had already wandered away into the forest.

Soon he came to the big oak tree under which they had eaten their picnic. 'I wonder if that squirrel who threw the acorn at Daisy is still there?' he thought.

At that moment *'plop'* there was an acorn on the grass in front of him. He looked up and staring down at him was a little grey face with twinkly eyes.

'Wait for me, Squirrel,' he called. 'I'm coming up there as well.' And he began to climb the tree.

Up and up through the branches he went. At last, with one last puff, he reached the squirrel.

'You can't climb trees as quickly as I can,' said Squirrel. 'No' agreed George, 'but I can do other things.' 'What sort of things?' asked the squirrel, very interested.

George thought. 'I can carry logs of wood' he said at last. 'Well,' said the squirrel, 'will you help me carry these acorns to my nest?' 'Certainly,' said George.

'Why are you gathering so many acorns?'
George wanted to know.

'It's food for my winter larder' was the
reply. 'I put a nice little pile of acorns
in a safe place then in winter I curl up
in my warm nest – which is called a drey – and
I sleep and sleep. But if I should wake up
and feel I need a snack, then I know just where
to find something tasty.'

But George wasn't really listening. He was staring down through the branches. 'Look there's my sister, Daisy. Shall we drop acorns on her to make her laugh?'

So they did. But Daisy didn't laugh at all. In fact 'Ooh Ooh!' she shrieked in alarm.

'George!' called father. 'I know you're up there. Come down at once!'

Two small faces – one grey and one brown – were looking down from the tree. 'Sorry, Daisy' said George but he was still laughing.

George began to climb down the tree and then he suddenly stopped. 'Father,' he called 'I can see some lovely blackberries! Can we go and pick them for mother?'

'Oh yes, please,' said Tim. 'Then we can have blackberry pie!'

'A good idea,'said father. 'Show us the way, George.'

George led the way to where he had seen the blackberries. 'There, look!' he said. There they were – shining and black and very beautiful.

'Oh I do so love blackberries,' cried Tim and he took a great mouthful of them. But then 'Oh they're horrible,' he cried. 'All sour and horrible!' and his face was screwed up like a brown paper bag.

George laughed so much he had to sit down.' You need to put sugar with them,' he said. 'Poor Tim!'

George led the way to where he had seen the blackberries.

They all picked the blackberries and
soon they had so many that the picnic
basket was quite full.

'Time to go home,' said father.
'We've done a good day's work and you've
all helped me very much.'

Tim and George carried the basket between
them and because there was no room for
Daisy on the sledge, she had a ride on father's
shoulders, holding very tightly to his ears.

They walked home rather slowly because
they were all tired, until in the distance
they saw lights shining through the shadows.

'It's our house,'said Tim. 'And there's
mother waiting for us,' said George.

But Daisy said nothing. She was fast
asleep, curled up like a small brown scarf
round father's neck.

Home for tea.

Mother Bear was delighted with the blackberries the children had picked.

'I shall be able to make lots of pies with these,' she said. 'Thank you very much, boys. Now if you would just put the logs in the shed you could have your bath afterwards.'

'When do we have something to eat?' asked George, anxiously. 'When you've had your bath,' said mother very firmly.

Now the boys had quite forgotten that the shed was a bit scary but as soon as they got to the door, they remembered.

'It's very dark in there' said George, peering in. 'Hm,' said Tim, 'why don't we just stand in the doorway and throw the logs in – then we needn't gg . . go right in.'

They threw in two logs then George said 'Stop it, Tim.' 'Stop what?' asked Tim. 'I'm not doing anything.' 'You're tickling my cheek,' growled George. 'No I'm not,'said Tim.

'Well something is' shrieked George – and they both got stuck in the doorway, trying to get out.

They held each other for comfort and
stared into the darkness.

'I felt something,' whispered George.
'It was terrible – sort of fluttery and
very very tickley . . .'

'It was only me,' said a very small voice.

Dangling in the doorway, swinging on
a thread, was a rather large spider.

'Oh Spider,' sighed George, 'you
really frightened me!'

'Sorry I'm sure,' giggled the spider.
'I was just spinning my web and swinging about and I suppose I touched your cheek by mistake. Quite by mistake of course!'

But George wasn't sure. He thought it quite possible that Spider had tickled him on purpose, especially as he heard him giggling as he scuttled away.

'I can't stand any more frights,' said Tim. As quickly as they could they threw the rest of the logs into the shed.

'Everyone's getting ready for winter,' said George. 'Dormouse is building a nest, Squirrel is gathering acorns and we're collecting wood.'

Just then they heard father calling. 'Time for your bath, boys,' he said.

'Thank goodness,' they both said and they ran back to the house as fast as their legs would carry them.

The bathroom was warm and steamy. Tim got in the bath then George squirted in the bubble bath. But he squirted so much that the bubbles floated up to the ceiling where they burst with soft little plops.

When George got in with Tim they played at submarines. This meant lying flat with just your nose sticking up and tickling each other's toes under water.

'That's funny,' said George, after a while, 'there's not much water in the bath.' 'That's because most of it is on the floor' Tim said.

'Tea's ready,'called mother from downstairs.

'Hooray!' said George and he got out of the bath so quickly that *'Crash!'* he slipped on the wet floor and got his head stuck in the waste paper basket.

Well, of course,Tim laughed and laughed.

– 'there's not much water in the bath' –

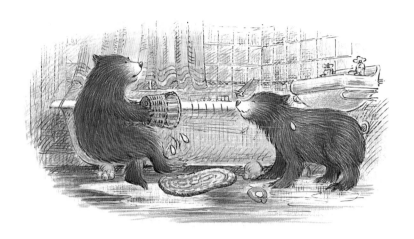

'Get me out of here,' called George.
'I'm stuck!'

Tim gave the basket a good tug. It came off George's head so suddenly that now it was Tim's turn to sit down – and George's turn to laugh.

'What's going on up here?' asked father, putting his head round the door. 'Oh boys, boys, what a *mess!* Now you can just clear it all up!'

They did their best. They mopped away (and sometimes slapped each other with wet cloths when father wasn't looking) and soon the bathroom was tidy – almost.

'That's better,' said father. 'Now at last we can go downstairs and have our tea.'

In front of a warm fire, the table was laid for tea. There were boiled eggs and brown toast, and small iced buns with cherries on top.

And in each place there was a new woolly hat: red for Tim, blue for George and a stripey one for Daisy made with the bits left over.

'I made them this afternoon,' said mother, 'so that your heads will be warm in winter.'

They all liked their hats so much that they put them on at once and wore them while they were having tea.

Their hard work in the forest had made them very hungry and soon all the plates on the table were empty.

'I hope you've left room for something special,' said mother. She went into the kitchen and came back carrying something very carefully. On to the table she put the most delicious looking pie. It was brown and crusty and shining with sugar.

'I made it with the blackberries you picked for me,' she said.

When the pie dish was empty and the last crusty bits scraped out (it was Tim's turn to scrape the dish) they pulled their chairs closer to the fire and father read them their bedtime story.

But the fire was so warm and their tummies so full and father's voice was so deep and rumbling – just like an old bee buzzing among summer flowers – that soon their heads began to nod. 'They're fast asleep' said mother.

They carried them upstairs and tucked them into bed and soon there was no sound except the soft breathing of three small bears, now fast asleep – and even in their sleep they would know that when the white snows of winter covered the great wood they would be safe and warm, all together, in their own cosy home.